The Legend of the Laughing Gecko

A Hawaiian Fantasy

Written and illustrated
by
Bruce Hale

Geckostufs, Inc. • Honolulu, Hawaii

This book is dedicated to the Aloha Spirit of the Hawaiian people.

A major mahalo to Brian Reed, Richard Brown, Marie Reiko Koch and Earl Chapman, whose generous spirit and aloha helped make this book a reality.

Glossary of Hawaiian Words:

Ali'i — (Ah-lee-ee) Hawaiian nobility
'Aumakua — (Ah-oo-ma-koo-ah) Animal spirit guardian, or "guardian angel"
Bufo — (Boo-fo) Hawaiian toad
'Ilio — (Ee-lee-oh) Dog
'Io — (Ee-oh) Hawk
Kahuna — (Ka-hoo-na) Wise man or priest
Pua'a — (Poo-ah-ah) Pig
Pueo — (Poo-eh-oh) Owl

Library of Congress Catalog Card Number 88-82098
ISBN: 0-9621280-0-7

Printed in Hong Kong

Deep in the heart of the blue Pacific Ocean, in the days before ice cream sundaes and color TV, the Hawaiian people lived in harmony with the animals.

One day, the king and queen called together all the animals and all the people for a special meeting. This was to be the great 'Aumakua Choosing, when each family would choose its 'aumakua, or sacred guardian animal.

It is on that day our story takes place.

The peace of a soft Hawaiian morning was shattered by the laugh of a gecko. "Oh, it's that Moki again," said Nene Goose, covering her ears.

"I do wish that boy would shut up," said the dog, Mrs. 'Ilio, to her husband. "He sounds awful!"

It was true. Moki the Gecko had a laugh that could shake the leaves off the trees or frighten the fish in the sea. His laugh bothered the Bufo toads. It irritated Pua'a the pig.

It even worried Moki's parents. "Son, tonight is the night of the 'Aumakua Choosing," said his mother. "It's a very important night. You won't embarrass us, will you?"

"What she means, Moki, is that you'd better keep a lid on that laugh of yours tonight," his father warned. "This is serious business.

"When our human brothers each choose an animal to watch over their families, you want some noble Ali'i family to pick us, don't you?"

Moki gulped and stammered, "Y-y-yes, sir."

"That's good, son. Remember, don't let us down. Now, run along and play until we're ready to go."

"Quietly," his mother added.

Within half an hour, Moki was laughing again, trading jokes with his friend, Pueo the owl.

"Okay, I've got one," chuckled Pueo. "Where does a 400-pound Bufo sleep?"

"Anywhere he wants to!" they shouted out together. Both animals rolled on the ground giggling. At Moki's supersonic laugh, three snails shrank back in their shells and a small protea plant turned pure white.

"Oh, Pueo, this is fun!" cried Moki. "But I've got to be serious tonight. Will you help me?"

"Don't worry, my friend," said Pueo. "I'll be right there beside you."

As the sun hung low, all humans and animals started towards the beach where the 'Aumakua Choosing would take place. Birds flew, pigs waddled and toads hopped from all over the islands.

Even the dolphins and butterfly fish swam up close to shore to join the meeting.

In fact, the only animal who wasn't there was the Black Bufo, a giant, poisonous toad who was nobody's friend and wouldn't have come if they'd asked him, anyway.

When all animals and humans had arrived, the Hawaiians' oldest kahuna (wise man) stepped into the circle and raised his hands. The crowd fell silent.

The kahuna sang a long chant to bring blessings onto the 'Aumakua Choosing. He warned everybody, human and animal, to stay perfectly quiet during the Choosing. He shook his magical gourd rattle.

And the Choosing began.

The king and queen rose, walked slowly around the circle and chose 'Io, the hawk, for their family's 'aumakua. In turn, the father and mother of another noble family got up and selected Pua'a the pig.

But when Moki saw the next father and mother stand up, he had to clap his hand over his mouth to hold in a laugh. The man looked like the 400-pound Bufo that Moki and Pueo had joked about earlier.

The more Moki tried not to think of Pueo's joke — have you ever tried *not* to think of something? — the more he thought about it. Moki looked up at Pueo, who was trying to keep a straight face, too.

That did it. In a flash, Moki burst out laughing, with a loud "Hee hee hee ho hoooo!"

The council stopped dead. People and animals covered their
ears or sat open-mouthed in shock.

The old kahuna whirled on the gecko family, pointing his finger. "You!" he shouted. "You geckos have broken our sacred silence. Now, go! Leave the circle."

Moki jumped up.
"It's all my fault!" he cried. "Now my family will never be 'aumakua. I ruined everything!"
And he ran off into the night alone.

Moki ran far into the forest, stumbling over roots, trying to outrun his tears. At last, he tripped and fell beside a moonlit pool. Moki burst out crying.

As he lay there in tears, Moki heard a branch crack behind him. He turned quickly in fright. Who knew what strange monsters lurked in that midnight forest?

Then, before his eyes, a little girl stepped out of the bushes.

"Who are you?" asked Moki.

"My name is Noelani. That means 'mist of heaven,'" she said. "I'm the king's youngest daughter.

"They wouldn't let me go to the Choosing because I'm too little. So I sneaked out of our hut to find it," she continued, "and I got lost.

"Why are you crying, little gecko?"

Moki told her about his terrible day — about joking with Pueo and being kicked out of the Choosing.

"And now I can't go home," he finished. "My parents will never forgive me."

"Oh, I don't know," said Noelani. "One time, I cut up Father's best fishing net to make a dress for my doll. He was so angry, I thought he would leave me in the forest for the Black Bufo to get me.

"I thought Father would never forgive me. But he did."

Moki said nothing, thinking about how much he missed his parents.

"I bet your parents are worried about you," Noelani said.

"I bet they are," Moki agreed. "But how can I face them after letting them down like that?"

"Just tell them you're sorry and that you love them," said Noelani. "That's all you can do. Come on, let's look for the path. I'll go with you."

They walked off into the forest together, searching for the way home. The moon hid behind a cloud and the forest grew darker and darker. The night was full of strange sounds.

Suddenly, Moki and Noelani stepped around a huge old tree and there he was — the Black Bufo. The two travelers froze in terror. The Black Bufo had big red eyes and a wide red mouth. His ugly black body was covered with warts that oozed poison.

"Well, what have we here?" he rumbled, "looks like dinner."

"Ulp," said Moki.

"Sounds like dinner," the Black Bufo smiled a terrible smile.

"Uh, we've got to go," said Noelani. She tried to scoot around the huge toad. But a big black-webbed foot shot out and pinned her down.

"Not so fast," snarled the Black Bufo.

Moki drew himself up to his full height and stared the Black Bufo in the face. "Let her go," he told the toad.

The creature only chuckled, an evil sound like old bones grinding.

"Look into my eyes," he commanded. Moki stared into the toad's huge red eyes. He was being hypnotized. He couldn't move, he couldn't look away.

The Black Bufo opened his jaws wide. "Come inside, little gecko," he said. "I promise you won't feel a thing."

Moki took one step towards the creature's open mouth and Noelani frantically tried to think how to save them both. But all she could think of was the silly joke that Pueo the Owl had told Moki.

In desperation, she shouted out: "Where does a 400-pound Bufo sleep? Anywhere he wants to!"

For an instant, nothing happened.

Then, Moki's lip twitched. His belly quivered. With a loud "hee hee hee ha hoooo!" he broke out of his trance and bounced around on the tip of his tail, laughing.

The Black Bufo stared in disbelief. A small croak escaped his lips. A rusty chuckle followed. The Black Bufo's face split in a wide grin and he joined the gecko's laughter with a booming "ho-ho-hoooo!"

Soon, he and Moki were rolling on the ground together, laughing like fools. Noelani leaned against a tree and giggled.

When he could talk again without laughing, the Black Bufo told Moki and Noelani his story.

Years ago, when the Black Bufo was small, he had lived with the other animals. But they always made fun of him and feared him because of his ugly body and sharp claws. Finally, they drove him away into the deep woods.

"Really, I'm not a bad guy," the toad said. "But nobody even gave me a chance to show it. After awhile, when everybody treats you like you're mean and evil, you start to believe it, too."

"But what about your poison warts?" asked Moki.

"So, I've got a bad skin condition," the toad said. "Would you hold that against me?"

After the three talked some more, the Black Bufo offered to guide his new friends back home, for it was very late. By the light of the sinking moon, they tramped through the dark woods.

I t was dawn when they came to Noelani's village. By this time, the king and queen had missed Noelani. They were forming a search party of the best warriors. Everybody gasped when Noelani and Moki rode into the village on a banana-leaf saddle, riding the Black Bufo.

"Look out — it's the Black Bufo and he's got my daughter!" cried the king.

"No, Father," said Noelani, jumping off the toad and running to
the king. "He's our friend now, thanks to Moki."

She hugged her mother and father. The villagers gathered around
while Noelani told of the night's adventures and how Moki's
laughter saved the day.

Moki's mother and father ran up and hugged him tight. The
kahuna walked up and apologized for kicking the geckos out of the
'Aumakua Choosing.

But the Choosing had finished hours ago. All Hawaiian families
had already picked their guardian animals and no family was left to
choose the geckos.

When Moki heard this, his face fell. He wanted so much for his
family to become someone's 'aumakua.

The queen said, "Moki, I'm sorry
the Choosing is over, but that's our law.
Not even the king and I can name you
geckos as one family's 'aumakua now."
The king kneeled. "But will you do us one
favor?" he asked. "Will you accept our
gratitude and deepest aloha for bringing
Noelani home safely?"
Moki nodded. He felt tears swell behind his eyes.
"Oh, and one more thing," the king said, "will you
accept for your family the position of 'aumakua
for all the islands of Hawai'i?"

Moki was so choked up, he could only nod "yes" at the great honor. The king rose.

"From this day forward, I declare the gecko to be official 'aumakua for all our islands," he shouted to his subjects.

The villagers sent up a great cheer. People and animals danced and sang, celebrating the gecko's triumph with music and laughter.

And Moki laughed loudest and longest of all.